May you always remember to embrace your uniqueness. Modunat & Ogunnaike &

Magic Crown
Copyright © 2021 Modinat Ogunnaike

Paperback ISBN: 978-1-7375096-8-4
Hardcover ISBN: 978-1-7375096-9-1

Editor: Crystal S. Wright
Zoë's T-shirt Graphic: By Cherie's Arts 'N Crafts

10 9 8 7 6 5 4 3 2 1
Printed in the United States

Priceless Publishing®
Coral Springs, Fl
www.pricelesspublishing.co

CONTENTS

DEDICATION

I dedicate this book to my loving mother & late father,
my siblings, friends, my husband and amazing daughters
Kemi & Adeola known as the O girls.

Last but not least to you the readers!
May you always remember to Embrace your uniqueness.

CHAPTER ONE

ZOË MEETS EMILY

Zoë! Zoë, wake up darling. Our new neighbors have finally arrived!"

I heard the sound of my Mom's voice wake me. I leaped out of bed with excitement, **"New neighbors, yay!"**

"I spotted a young girl your age. Maybe you two will be good friends," Momma said with a smile.

"Wow, really?"

I was even more eager to meet them. I ate breakfast quickly while Mom worked on the fruit basket welcome gift and Dad was getting ready for work.

"All done!" Mom shouted happily.

Finally, the basket was complete. It looked so perfect with the mixture of grapes, berries, apples, pears, watermelon, and bananas.

I grabbed my doll Emilee and dashed down the stairs to meet Momma.

Suddenly, the door was opened by a beautiful, tall lady with the most amazing curly hair. *"Hello, we are your next-door neighbors. My daughter and I wanted to gift your family with this small welcome basket."*

"Oh how kind of you. Thank you so much. This is my daughter Emily." I noticed a girl about my age peeking behind the lady, guess that's who Momma was talking about. Oh my God, did she just say Emily? I beamed with excitement. I waved to her and she waved back.

As Momma said her good byes, I handed Emily my doll with a big grin, *"This is my gift to you. Her name is Emilee too!"*

Emily smiled, **"Thank you so much, she's so pretty!"**

As we walked away, Momma said she was surprised that I gave my doll away. *"Zoë, that was very kind of you to do."*

Smiling, I replied, **"Well, Momma I wanted to give something to her."**

"Ok baby. Let's go get ready for your first day of school tomorrow.

CHAPTER TWO

RUN! I SAID RUN!

It was the first week of school and I couldn't wait to see my best friends, Tilly and Sophia. I met Tilly a few years ago in the 2nd grade and Sophia in the 3rd, and now we are all in 4th grade. We have all been close since day one.

As Momma pulled up to the school gate, I spotted them standing by our favorite tree. I hurriedly kissed Momma goodbye and hopped out of the car and ran to hug my two besties.

It was so good to see them again!

During recess, we met again underneath our favorite tree and chatted about our new teachers, and how the day was going so far. I then saw Emily, my new neighbor, looking so nervous. I called her over to hang with us.

"Hi Emily. It's me Zoë, your neighbor." She smiled and looked relieved to see a familiar face. I introduced her to Tilly and Sophia.

The last bell rang for school and like usual, Sophia, Tilly and I met at our favorite tree to walk home together. As soon as we stepped out of the school yard, it started to rain cats and dogs and none of us had an umbrella.

I squealed and put my hands on my head to shield my hair because I knew this fresh blowout from Momma was about to get soaked. I gave Tilly and Sophia a terrified look and I did the only thing I could do — RUN!

I immediately ran off, and yelled as they were walking casually, "RUN, I SAID RUN!"

We ran the rest of the way home. It felt like 50 miles!

As we made it to the front porch of my house, I saw Emily and her mom approaching their front door. I yelled out to Emily to join us for some hot cocoa and after school snacks with a piece of pound cake.

Emily looked up at her mom said a few words and came running across the yard. Funny enough the sun was shining so bright by this time. I guess it was just a quick rain shower.

As we entered the kitchen, Tilly immediately asked me why I had squealed so loudly when it started raining.

CHAPTER THREE

HAIR'S WHAT HAPPENED!

Tilly and Sophia had no clue but my hair is the reason why I squealed so loudly when it started raining. **MY HAIR'S WHAT HAPPENED!** I had to explain to them that my straightened hair changes immediately when water touches it and I really wanted to keep this style for at least the first week of school.

Emily chimed in, *"Oh my gosh, I was thinking the same thing. I was lucky my mom was waiting right outside the school for me in the car. I just prefer to not get my hair wet!"*

Emily had hair full of curls just like mine.

"Wow, are you kidding me? Do you know what I would do to get my hair to curl up or do something besides staying straight?" Sophia said.

Sophia is originally from Mexico and she has always had straight black hair down to her waist. She said *"I would love a little bounce to my hair"* Tilly giggled. Her family is from Ireland and she has amazing red ringlets as hair strands which was always so pretty to me. Not to forget her amazing freckles.

Tilly said, *"Guys, have you noticed that the things we are complaining about is what we love about one another. Like you Zoë, you and Emily don't like your beautiful curly hair getting wet because it changes the look. But Sophia, you wish that your hair would curl up when it gets wet. As for me, you guys always say how much you love my red hair and freckles, but I don't always love it. Being called 'connect the dots face' is not fun."*

Everyone was silent as they sipped their hot chocolate. We were deep in thought. We chatted a little more before it was time for the girls to head home and start our first day homework assignments. As I was getting ready to start my homework, Momma walked by and said she overheard us talking about our hair and things that we are not too happy about.

"Baby, I want you to know something."

"What, Momma?"

"Zoë, do you know that you are magic?"

"Magic? What do you mean momma?"

"Baby, your hair is your crown. You are filled with magic and your crown is one of the visible pieces of magic. I want you to always wear your crown with pride and confidence whether it's wet, straight, dry, curly or in pigtails. Whichever way you wear it, it's MAGIC!" She squeezed me tight and kissed my forehead.

CHAPTER FOUR

MAGIC CROWNS

It was a bright Saturday morning and I knew Tilly and Sophia would be ringing the doorbell any minute now to ride our bikes. As I headed to the garage to get my bike, I saw Emily playing jax with her mother so I rushed over there.

 "Wow, jax! My mother talks about this game all the time and how growing up it was one of her favorite things to do on the weekend with her sisters."

Emily's mom was eager to teach me the tricks to bouncing the ball and picking up the jax pieces quickly. After a few minutes, I got the hang of it. By this time Sophia and Tilly were riding up to my house. I was so eager to share with them what my mom explained to me about our crowns. After riding down the street and back, we decided to take a break near my treehouse. It out back near Dad's shed.

"Guys, we are magic," I blurted with a big grin. They looked at each other confused.

Tilly was the first to speak. **"Umm Zoë, what are you talking about?"**

"My mom overheard us complaining yesterday about our hair. So, she explained to me that our hair is our magic crown! Whether it's curly, straight, wet or dry, we are all unique and we should be proud and confident no matter how it looks."

The girls were all excited to think that their hair is a crown and it's magic.

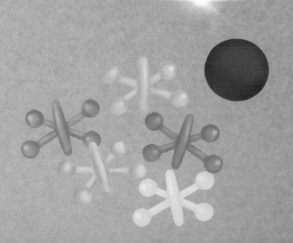

I said, *"Guys, let's make a pact that we will always remember how amazing, confident and beautifully magical we are, and wear our magic crown with pride."*

We held our hands together and shouted, *"MAGIC CROWNS!"*

Later on that evening Emily's mom called my mom to share how Emily has been beaming around the house talking about how magical she is and that she is so proud of her magic crown. My mom just chuckled and said, *"That's fantastic to hear. I wonder where she came up with that,"* as she winked at me.

She hung up the phone and then said to me, *"Zoë, I see that you shared with your friends the magic that you all wear everyday."*

"Mom thank you so much for explaining to me how amazing we all really are. It made me look at myself differently and love my hair even more."

I told her of the pact we made to always be proud of who we are and the hair that God gave us. I also told her that I'm actually looking forward to the next rain shower. We giggled and hugged.

The next day Tilly rang my doorbell and said, *"Zoë, I have a question."*

"My cousin Cara has something called Alopecia, and she doesn't have any hair. I wanted to share our pact with her, but then I remembered she doesn't have any hair because of her condition.

So my question is, does that mean she's not magical since she doesn't have any hair…you know her magic crown?"

Zoë looked puzzled.

"Tilly, I don't know. Why don't you ask my mom.

Mom!"

MAGIC CROWN MANTRA

I AM BEAUTIFUL

I AM UNIQUE

I AM CONFIDENT

I AM INTELLIGENT

I AM MAGIC

ABOUT THE AUTHOR

MODINAT OGUNNAIKE, affectionately known as Mrs. O, is a Nigerian American born and raised in New Jersey. She still lives in the state today with her husband and two daughters. Magic Crown is only one of many outlets where Modinat's passion will be shared with the world.

Modinat has served in the social services field for over 14 years, continuing the rich tradition of her other family members. She is cofounder of InTouch Wellness, a successful life coaching and self development company with her siblings where they help their clients maximize their potential.

Mrs. O enjoys traveling, reading and writing, and dabbles in interior designing. She has used her eye for style to create Shollyo's Bows, which features a unique line of hair adornments for women and young girls. Passionate about volunteerism and young people, she displays this commitment through her local Big Brother/Sister program, church and greater community where she mentors youth.

All these passions and hobbies fade in comparison to raising her daughters which gives Modinat the greatest sense of fulfillment. She looks forward to continuing to influence and have a positive impact among the new generation of young women, and hopes that her contributions teach them to be bold and confident in who they are.

CPSIA information can be obtained
at www.ICGtesting.com
Printed in the USA
BVHW020320071221
622100BV00002B/12

* 9 7 8 1 7 3 7 5 0 9 6 9 1 *